THE TESTERS

The Poison Remembers

GENE SCOTT

Edited by
GEORGIA AUSTIN

ALSO BY GENE SCOTT

Jellybeaners (2017)

The Water Remembers (2025)

Debra's Song (2025)

THE TESTERS

CONTENTS

In every court, in every century, someone profits from poison.

And someone must stand between the chalice and the crown.

— Tester's Proverb, Circa 1521

PROLOGUE

Hampton Court Palace – May Fifteenth, 1521

First Taste

The wine touches my tongue, and I know.

Foxglove—masked beneath Spanish muscatel—bitter as betrayal. Metallic undertones bloom across taste buds long scarred by survival. Copper rides in on sweetness like a knife sheathed in velvet.

Three heartbeats. Four. Still standing.

Across the candlelit din of the Hall of Presence, I meet Margaret's eyes. Her fingers work dried yarrow in her apron pocket. I see the tension in her shoulders—how she's already read the room, the rim of the goblet, the page's trembling hand.

Someone here wants the king dead.

And they're willing to kill me to do it.

My name is Thomas Tester. My family does not rule, or pray, or heal for coin.

We taste for poison.

Born in the shadow of Black Mountain—where Wales meets England's edge, where wild things cling to stone—I was raised to swallow danger before others sip. My grandmother taught me the difference between healing and harm the way other boys learned hymns.

She pressed diluted belladonna to my lips when I was seven. "Feel that burn?" she whispered. "Good. That's your body learning to live."

I wept blood and bile for two days. But I lived.

Men like Bainbridge call this concoction medicine when they administer it. Witchcraft when women do. Tonight, it's neither.

Tonight, it's murder. And I've just swallowed it.

Behind Harrington's thin smile, Thomas Boleyn watches like a man who's already measured my coffin. These wolves have circled for weeks —sniffing weakness ever since Anne caught the king's wandering gaze. Court politics sharpen faster than knives.

Harrington lifts his own goblet, feigning camaraderie. "A fine vintage, wouldn't you say, Master Tester?"

The poison licks its way down my throat. My gut clenches, but I smile. I have to.

To spit at the king's table would get me beheaded faster than the foxglove can work.

My son Edward watches from the gallery—eight years old, eyes too old for his face. I will not let him see me fall.

Margaret's hum threads the noise—soft, steady, a Welsh healing song no one else here would recognize. It's our tether. Our ward. I feel it in my bones, in my breath, in the ache of muscle resisting collapse.

We prepared for this.

Beneath the floorboards of our quarters lie elderberry tinctures gathered in secret, hawthorn to calm a failing heart, charcoal for drawing poison. Remedies passed mouth to mouth for generations— never inked on parchment, never trusted to the hands of men who burn knowledge once they've stolen it.

I sip again.

Because a Tester does not flinch. We do not panic. We buy time for the antidote to reach our blood. We play our part until the danger passes—or kills us.

Some families test metals for kings.

We test death.

The only question is whether I survive this cup . . .

. . . or whether my son inherits a legacy of sacrifice without understanding its cost.

Because in every court, in every century, someone profits from poison.

And someone must stand between the chalice and the crown.

Chapter One

STORIES THAT WON'T STAY BURIED

Carter County, Tennessee — March Fifteenth, 2025

Mist clings to my grandmother's headstone like breath refusing to leave the body.

I trace the carved dates: born sixty-two years ago, died three months before I could drag the truth into the light. The coroner called it an accidental overdose.

I know better.

I press wild yarrow to the granite. Its scent rises sharp and bitter, cutting through the fog. The same herb she tucked in her pockets, in her medicine pouches, beneath the mattresses of the people she tried to save. Painkiller, fever-fighter, spirit-clearer. Now it's an offering.

"I found the files," I whisper. "The ones they tried to bury."

The wind shifts like someone listening.

Two whistleblowers are already dead. One "fell asleep at the wheel." The other overdosed on his own research chemicals—convenient, considering his final report accused Northeastern Medical of falsifying addiction data.

I have their notes. Their access codes. Their ghosts riding shotgun every time I sit down at my computer.

This week, I testify before the state oversight committee. The data

I've recovered—clinical trials, internal emails, dosage schedules—could spark criminal investigations. Maybe even shut them down.

If I survive long enough to deliver it.

The university medical building gleams across the foothills, white and sharp as a scalpel. Funded by the same pharmaceutical conglomerate that buried Grandma with a double dose of prescribed dependency.

They call this progress. In these hills, we know better.

This is extraction, dressed up in lab coats.

The parking lot is empty—it's a Saturday. My office lights flicker on as I swipe my badge. I should be home. But I need to work. To organize the files, encrypt the records, prepare for what comes next.

But before I touch the handle, I know.

Someone's been here.

The air smells wrong. Like pine cleaner covering expensive cologne. Like someone rich tried to erase their presence. But I smell intention.

My desk is too neat. The death certificates—three twenty-five-year-olds—are laid out with surgical care. Each one has a photo clipped: Jessica Winters, Marcus Tillery, Amber Collins. All local. All started on Northeastern Medical's "non-addictive" painkillers after workplace injuries. All overdosed last weekend.

These aren't statistics. These are people I know.

Jessica's mother reads to my cousin's kids at the library. Marcus played ball with Caleb before the accident shattered his spine. Amber's daughter lives three doors down from my Aunt Ruth Ann.

Grief connects us in these mountains like creek beds—on the surface, visible. But it runs deeper.

The pharmaceutical rep steps into my doorway like he owns the oxygen in the room.

Harrison. Tailored suit. Factory smile. No calluses on his hands. His presence smells like entitlement and aftershave.

"Dr. Grace Blackwood," he says, rolling the title like it's temporary. "Your research raises . . . concerns about our marketing practices."

My hand tightens around the flash drive in my pocket. The access codes stored there lead to three years of buried data—proof of targeting, of manipulation, of chemical weaponry disguised as care.

"You're emotionally involved with Caleb Tester, aren't you?" he asks casually, already flipping the blade.

There it is.

The word he wants to carve me with.

Addict.

As if that's the whole story. As if Caleb's crushed vertebrae, seven months of sobriety, and the legacy of mountain healing wrapped around his spine mean nothing. As if discrediting my relationship discredits the truth.

I keep my voice steady. "Three kids died last weekend from prescriptions your reps pushed. You tracked how many pills you could ship before raising federal red flags."

"You're treading close to professional misconduct," he warns. "Your tenure review is next week, isn't it?"

He places a manila envelope on my desk with a manicured hand.

Inside: surveillance photos. Me and Caleb at NA meetings. Me at his family's cabin. Moments twisted into ammunition.

Through the window behind him, the hills rise blue and knowing. These mountains remember every system that came to take—loggers, miners, factory bosses—and now this. Medicine made into a weapon.

"You're not from here," he says softly. "You're playing mountain savior. We see that type a lot."

Wrong again.

My grandmother taught me to read the ridges like scripture. She taught me what to plant for bleeding and what to burn for bad spirits. Her yarrow still grows along my porch. Her blood is mine.

I smile, slow and sharp. "Your company's not the first to underestimate mountain people. It won't be the last to regret it."

My phone buzzes.

Caleb: *Found something in Grandpa's papers. Older than Prohibition. Testers before we were even Testers. Come quick. Don't tell anyone.*

I stand, gather the files, the photos, the names of the dead.

Harrison doesn't move. "Some stories," he says, "should stay buried."

I walk past him, spine straight, voice calm. "And some truths don't rot easy. Not here."

Outside, the wind has picked up. The creek sings louder than it did this morning. The yarrow at Grandma's grave felt different too—like it knew what was coming.

This isn't just a research paper anymore.

This is testimony.

And the mountains are listening.

Chapter Two

THE PRICE OF KNOWLEDGE

Hampton Court Palace – May Sixteenth, 1521

I wake to the scent of blood and elderberries.

Margaret crushes the berries in her mortar, her fingers raw where the juice seeps into a fresh cut. Purple stains streak her skin like war paint. Light from the high windows slants across hanging herbs—foxglove, henbane, monkshood—each one lethal if the wrong eyes take notice.

My limbs tremble beneath sweat-soaked linen. The poison hasn't left me yet. My stomach churns. My pulse kicks behind my eyes.

"Edward," I rasp. "Did they question him?"

Margaret doesn't look up. "They did. Then let him go."

"And Harrington?"

She snorts. "Still lapping wine like it wasn't meant to kill you."

The air in our chambers carries tension like storm pressure. Every shadow could be a spy. Every knock could be a summons or a sentence.

Margaret's eyes are ringed in sleepless gray. Her hands don't tremble as she adds dried snakeroot to the mixture. Her calm frightens me more than panic would.

"The Boleyns are aligning with Harrington," she says quietly. "Anne asked me to serve as her personal herbalist."

My throat closes. "You refused."

"I said I'd consider it." Her eyes meet mine, steady as iron. "We need allies, Thomas."

"She'll use you and discard you."

"Like the king uses you?"

Silence falls between us, sharp and sudden. My pride aches more than my poisoned gut.

"I haven't slept," she mutters, voice cracking. "Forgive me."

This court eats loyalty for breakfast.

We came here to protect, to use what we knew to prevent suffering. Instead, we're drowning in velvet-draped danger and silver-tongued betrayal. Margaret once gathered herbs in moonlight for healing. Now she hides them like weapons.

She presses a cool cloth to my forehead. I breathe her in—smoke, rosemary, the faint scent of earth after rain. Our language is touch. Pressure. Presence. She doesn't need to speak to say what she fears:

We are running out of time.

Chapter Three

THE COST OF SILENCE

Carter County, Tennessee – March Fifteenth, 2025 – Three O'Clock A.M.

My phone buzzes on the nightstand.

I don't answer right away.

The mountains outside my window are breathing—thin clouds sliding across their ribs like smoke. Moonlight silvering the ridgelines. Somewhere, an owl calls.

The phone buzzes again. The name on the screen: **Harrison**.

Third call tonight.

I pick up. Don't speak.

His voice slithers through the line. "Dr. Blackwood. I hope I didn't wake you."

"I don't sleep much anymore."

A pause. A smile I can hear. "We're concerned. You're preparing some . . . inflammatory material for your testimony Thursday."

I stare out the window. "I'm preparing the truth."

"Some truths," he says, "aren't meant for public consumption."

Another pause. "Roads get treacherous in these hills. Accidents happen. People disappear."

I've heard that kind of threat before—but never directed at me.

Still, I say nothing.

Let silence do the talking.

Let him wonder what I've already shared, what I've already backed up.

He continues. "You're an intelligent woman. You don't want to end up like Walker."

My stomach turns to ice. "Dr. Walker's overdose was listed as accidental."

"So was your grandmother's."

My breath stops.

He knows.

Downstairs, the house creaks. Too heavy for the wind. I grab my laptop. The flash drive. My encrypted notes.

I hear it now—the real reason Harrison called. A distraction while someone searches my office. Or waits outside.

I move fast, quiet. Years in the mountains taught me how to walk without waking the ground.

I slip out the back, through the trees.

Branches scrape my coat. Cold air bites.

I keep moving until I reach the service road that cuts behind the biology building.

Campus security doesn't patrol here, but Ruth Ann does.

She's waiting beside her truck, already lit a cigarette, already knows why I'm here.

"Figured you'd come."

She tosses a blanket over my laptop bag, eyes scanning the tree line.

"There's residue on your windowsill," she says. "Powdered alkaloid. You got watched."

I nod. "He mentioned Grandma."

She exhales smoke like a curse. "Then it's started."

We slip into the truck, and she drives without headlights for the first quarter mile. She knows every turn by feel.

"When Jenny died," she says finally, voice flat, "they said it was misuse."

I nod. Jenny's overdose was the one that broke Ruth Ann open. Broke her quiet. Made her dangerous.

"She was trying to wean off," Ruth Ann continues. "Used the herbs.

Logged everything. She was tracking how they increased her dosage every refill."

"She left notes?"

"In her baby's books. Inside the covers. Herbal margins." Her voice tightens. "They made sure she got the strong batch that last time."

The road disappears into trees. Fog slithers low, hugging the ground.

"They've done this before," I whisper. "Suppressed data. Targeted vulnerable counties. Paid off researchers. Buried whistleblowers."

"And now they've got you." Ruth Ann looks over. "Unless we move first."

My phone vibrates again. A text from Caleb:

Found something in Grandpa's shed. Pre-Prohibition. Older. Welsh. Cherokee. "Testers" before we were Testers. Get here. Don't talk to anyone.

I stare at the message like it's a doorway.

Something's waiting on the other side. Not just evidence. Legacy. Proof of what we've always known but couldn't always show:

We were here first. We were healing before they called it witchcraft. We were protecting each other before they patented pain.

We crest a ridge. Ruth Ann slows.

"Brake line was cut," she says quietly. "Your car. I checked it earlier."

She doesn't look at me.

And I don't ask how she knew to look.

Mountain women don't need permission to protect what's theirs.

In the distance, lights flicker on the Tester land. The mountains lean close.

"We still going?" she asks.

I clutch the flash drive tighter. Inside it: the names of the dead. The dosage trails. The marketing maps where red Xs mark the counties with the most injured workers—and the fewest doctors.

Inside it: truth they'll kill for.

"We're going," I say.

Ruth Ann nods once, then drives us down into the dark.

Somewhere behind us, someone's erasing files. Scrubbing footage. Preparing headlines for the next "unfortunate overdose."

But ahead of us, in an old shed built with cedar and secrets, something waits.

Something older than this war.

Something that remembers.

Chapter Four

POISON AND POWER

Hampton Court Palace – May Seventeenth, 1521

The boy dies before dawn.

Lord Pembroke, fifteen years old, heir to a fortune and a father's ambition, bleeds from the nose before the first bell tolls and seizes in his bed before a prayer can reach his lips.

The physicians call it imbalance. Bad humors. Perhaps a chill.

But I know belladonna when I see it.

I sit in the corner of the chamber while Bainbridge performs his ritual—checking the boy's pulse, tongue, temperature—knowing full well what he'll find. A line of courtiers crowds the hallway, murmuring about spirits and sin, as if confession can cure poison.

No one looks at me.

But they all know why I'm here.

They know I tasted the king's wine two nights ago and lived.

They wonder if this death means I failed.

They wonder if I chose to.

Margaret finds me kneeling in the chapel hours later, hands resting on cold stone. I haven't prayed in years, but silence sometimes feels like enough.

She doesn't speak at first, just stands beside me, close enough to feel the heat radiating off my skin.

Finally, she says, "The boy wasn't the target."

"No."

"And yet."

I nod. "And yet."

Margaret's presence steadies me. I hear the rustle of her skirts, the faint clink of a charm hidden beneath her bodice—yarrow, rosemary, angelica root.

She always carries protection.

We've needed it more since the Boleyns began circling like vultures dressed in silk.

"Bainbridge says you might've saved him," she says.

"Did he?"

She nods. "Claims your 'peasant remedies' might've countered the poison."

"Interesting. He mocked those same remedies last month, right before ordering more poppy tincture for his sleep."

She gives a humorless laugh. "Now he wants what we have. Knowledge—without the blood."

We sit beneath the vaulted ceiling, where saints stare down at sinners with carved pity.

"They're watching Edward," she says at last.

My spine stiffens. "Who?"

"Cromwell. Harrington. The Boleyn girl's maid mentioned him by name. They've heard he knows herbs."

Of course they have. He speaks like a child but listens like a spy. They see a prodigy. A tool. A weakness.

"They'll want him in their service next," I say. "Train him young. Cut him from us before he remembers who he is."

"Like they did to your cousin."

I flinch.

"Thomas," she says, sharper now, "if something happens—"

"Don't." Her voice slices clean. "Don't speak like a man preparing to die."

We've always known this day would come.

At court, survival isn't luck. It's strategy. Silence. Knowing when to heal and when to let the poison run its course.

We've survived by hiding truth in plain sight.

In recipes.

In lullabies.

In our son.

She places a leather-wrapped charm in my hand, still warm from her skin.

"Angelica. Hawthorn. Ash," she says. "For protection. Wear it beneath your clothes. Don't let them see you carry it."

I close my fingers around it.

Later, I find Edward in the corner of our quarters, reading a book that looks like scripture.

But I know better.

I sit beside him.

"Do you understand what happened to Lord Pembroke?" I ask.

He nods.

"Will you tell me?"

"He drank milk with honey," he says softly. "They say it was the nursemaid's idea. But she's new. And the honey came from Harrington's estate."

He's eight.

And already, he sees what others can't.

"Did you touch the book?" I ask.

He doesn't answer.

I open my palm. The spiral-carved stone rests inside.

"You're not ready," I say.

"I might need to be," he answers.

God help us. He might be right.

I tuck the stone back into its pouch. Brush his hair from his forehead. His skin is warm, taut with tension.

"Today, you study rosemary and mint. Nothing more."

His lips tighten. He always wants more.

There's a knock at the door.

Not polite. Not hesitant.

A summons.

Margaret opens it.

Cromwell stands on the threshold, eyes like slate, hands folded behind his back.

"The queen has requested a review of the court's wine stores," he says. "All chalices must be verified. The king requires your expertise."

His tone says what his words don't:

We don't trust anyone now.

Least of all the man who keeps surviving.

Behind me, Edward reaches for the feverfew he picked yesterday.

Just in case.

Chapter Five

THE BLOOD LEDGER

Carter County, Tennessee — March Fifteenth, 2025 — 5:49 A.M.

By the time I reach the old Tester property, the sky has turned the color of bruised stone.

Fog moves like breath between the trees. A crow watches me from a sagging fence post, and for one irrational moment, I nod to it like it's a sentinel.

It doesn't blink.

I step over the chain gate and follow the rutted gravel path past the old barn, the slope-shouldered smokehouse, and the chicken coop that hasn't held a bird since Caleb's grandfather died.

At the edge of the woods stands the shed.

The place he wasn't supposed to enter. The place his grandfather always kept locked. The place holding the truth we weren't ready for.

Caleb stands in the open doorway like a man who's touched the past and come away changed.

He's barefoot, in jeans and a thermal shirt, hair damp from sweat or fog. He doesn't look up right away—just stares down at the open crate in front of him like it's a grave he unearthed by accident.

"Morning," I say softly.

His shoulders lift on a breath. "You came."

"You texted: 'don't tell anyone, bring the ledgers.' That's not a request. That's prophecy."

He smiles—just barely—but it doesn't reach his eyes.

"Inside," he says.

The shed smells like cedar, dust, and secrets.

A single lantern glows from a hook. In its light, I see what he's found: oilskin-wrapped bundles, glass vials with faded labels, a set of copper tasting spoons, and at the bottom—a journal bound in tooled leather, its edges crumbling, its pages inked in a language that doesn't belong to any one country.

Welsh consonants. Cherokee vowels. A rhythm that belongs to this land and nowhere else.

I kneel beside him. My fingers hover above the journal before I touch it.

"The handwriting's different than the ledgers," I whisper.

"It's older," he says. "The ones in the house start around 1918. This . . ." He looks at me. "This was written before statehood. Maybe before maps even reached these hollows."

I flip the page.

The ink is iron-black, faded at the edges. There are diagrams of plants with roots that twist like snakes and annotations that read more like incantations than recipes.

"This isn't just healing," I murmur. "This is . . . decoding harm."

One passage stops me cold.

It's a tasting guide. Not for wine. For poisons.

Foxglove tastes of copper and rain. Hemlock like green almonds in spring. Belladonna whispers sweet before it bites.

Taste the lies before they speak them. Know the difference between pain and ending.

Testers must carry the truth before they give it.

A shiver ripples through me.

This is what they did. They didn't just heal the sick. They protected the living from the deadliest lies in the world.

Caleb crouches beside another crate. Pulls out a stack of wax-sealed envelopes.

"One of these had his name," he says. "Grandpa Ezra. The seal's the same spiral carved into the stone you gave me."

He holds it out.

I break the seal with shaking fingers.

Inside, a single sheet—faded handwriting in Ezra Tester's careful print.

If you're reading this, it means someone finally came looking for the truth.

They'll come for you now. They always do.

But remember—what kills in excess heals in measure.

What they call witchcraft is science they haven't earned.

What they fear is memory.

Use it.

I swallow the lump rising in my throat.

This isn't folklore. It's a blueprint.

These journals weren't just kept. They were hidden—preserved like seed corn beneath winter ash. Waiting for the next generation to break the silence open.

"Someone cut my brake line," I say.

Caleb looks up sharply. His knuckles tighten against the crate's rim.

"Then it's started."

"Ruth Ann says Jenny was keeping records too," I add. "Inside her kids' books. That she was teaching her baby about plants the week she died."

His jaw flexes. He nods once, hard.

"Then it's not just history," he says. "It's a pattern."

He pulls out a glass vial, the liquid inside the color of moonlight on bone.

"Do you know what this is?" he asks.

I shake my head.

"It's from my great-great-grandmother. Eleanor Walkingstick. The label's in the hybrid script. I ran it through AI last year, just for fun. Want to know what the algorithm called it?"

"What?"

"Memory protection."

I exhale slowly. "Not sure the machine was wrong."

I pull out my laptop. Fire it up. Open the files. Caleb kneels beside me.

We sync what he's found with what I've downloaded: patient maps, opioid targeting patterns, overdoses by region.

Side by side, century-old poison ledgers and modern pharmaceutical spreadsheets line up like soldiers.

Their methods changed. Their goal never did.

Profit from pain. Silence the ones who know better.

Outside, the wind picks up.

Inside, the truth breathes louder.

We've found the fuse.

The question is how long we have before someone lights it.

Chapter Six

SECOND TASTING

Hampton Court Palace – May Eighteenth, 1521

The goblet gleams in the light of thirty tapers. Polished silver. Royal crest etched into its side. Elegant. Deadly.

I take it with hands that still tremble.

The king watches from his dais, golden robe puddled around him like a lion too lazy to hunt. His face is flushed, wine-blown. But his eyes are sharp. He's waiting.

Not for the taste.

For the decision.

I raise the goblet. Tilt. Sip.

And wait for death to introduce itself again.

This time, it tastes like cinnamon.

But underneath—there it is. That wrongness. That heat coiled like a snake behind the sweetness.

Clove? No. Something sharper.

Three heartbeats.

Four.

The hall holds its breath with me.

I lower the goblet. My pulse hammers in my throat. A bead of sweat slides down my spine.

"Acceptable," I say, voice steady. "The vintage is clean."

A lie.

It's not clean. But it's not lethal—yet.

Margaret's tincture waits beneath my tongue, a measured dose of crushed angelica and elderflower to hold back the worst.

The king smiles, baring teeth. "Marvelous. See, Lord Harrington? I told you this Tester had a rare palate."

The courtiers laugh like trained dogs. Harrington doesn't. He tips his goblet to me with a smile that never reaches his eyes.

Behind him, Anne Boleyn whispers something to her maid, eyes flicking toward Margaret, who stands near the back with the other herbal attendants.

A new game is starting.

And we are both pieces on the board.

After the ceremony, I stagger through the side corridors—ancient stone pressing in, shadows thicker than smoke. I lean against a pillar, breathing through the fire in my gut.

Margaret finds me there, wordless, already slipping a vial into my palm.

"I counted the notes," she says. "Too much nutmeg in the mix. It wasn't Harrington's wine alone. Someone added spice after the pour."

"So a test," I whisper.

"To see what you'd taste. To see if you'd lie."

I unscrew the vial and swallow the contents. It burns. Then cools. Then settles.

Like fear turned to resolve.

We retreat to our chambers in silence.

When the door closes, we exhale.

"I heard something," Margaret says. "Anne Boleyn's maid talking to Cromwell."

"Go on."

"She said the king wants a 'legacy of testers.'"

I freeze.

"They're considering Edward," she adds. "As a ward. To train at court. As . . . insurance."

My blood turns to ice.

Not a gift.

Not an honor.

A leash.

Edward sits at the hearth, sorting thyme leaves into piles by size and color. He looks up at us, sees our faces, and knows something has shifted.

We taught him too well.

Later, I write in the hidden ledger beneath the floorboards. Ink smudges beneath my unsteady fingers.

Tested the king's wine. Spice blend masked undertones. Not fatal. Not yet. Intent unclear. Tincture from Margaret mitigated symptoms. Edward's name was spoken by Boleyn's maid. They are watching.

I pause.

I fear the boy will be claimed before he understands the weight of his name.

That night, I wake to footsteps in the corridor. Not hurried. Deliberate.

I rise.

At the door—a note pressed into the stone.

No wax. No seal. Just six words in the careful script of a court scribe:

Test again. This time, don't lie.

Chapter Seven

THE CIRCLE GATHERS

Carter County, Tennessee – March Sixteenth, 2025

The lights are out when I reach Dr. Walkingstick's cabin.

Not dark—off. As in, deliberately cut.

Ruth Ann's truck is already there, mud still wet on the tires. Inside the cabin, candles flicker low, throwing the walls into shifting patterns.

We're off-grid now.

Sarah Walkingstick opens the door, her face half-lit, half-shadow. Her braid falls over one shoulder, black streaked with gray, silver glinting like wire. She doesn't smile.

"Phones go in the freezer," she says.

No preamble. Just protocol.

Inside—it's like stepping into a different century.

Copper kettles. Dried herbs. Handwritten notes scrawled in Cherokee and cursive. A mortar sits on the table beside a battered laptop and a sealed box marked **TESTER — 1894**.

Ruth Ann stands near the hearth, arms folded. Caleb paces restlessly.

They've all seen the files.

They know what's coming.

I place the flash drive on the table. "It's not enough to expose them," I say. "We need to survive doing it."

"Survival's not passive," Sarah says. "It's a strategy."

She opens a tin of dried blue cohosh and scatters it onto the table. "For strength. For labor. For making pain birth something."

We go over the data.

Harrison's patterns.

Prescribing maps.

Hospital kickbacks.

But it's Caleb who brings the room to a hush.

He opens the 1894 box. Inside: a spiral-carved amulet and a sealed glass vial with hand-scratched text on the label.

Memory hold. For truth keepers only.

Sarah stares. "This is from Eleanor Walkingstick. My great-aunt."

Ruth Ann steps forward. "She worked with Ezra Tester during the TB outbreak. They knew the system would twist healing into control."

She looks at me. "Now it's your turn."

We form a plan.

Disseminate the files anonymously through a Cherokee environmental justice group.

Submit redacted evidence through my attorney.

Prepare a digital deadman's switch through Sarah's cousin, who builds privacy tools for whistleblowers.

"Still leaves one problem," Caleb says. "You."

Everyone looks at me.

"I'm the leak," I admit. "They'll come for me first."

Sarah hands me a bundle wrapped in cloth. "Wear this under your clothes. Plant warding. Salt-sewn edges. Don't take it off."

Ruth Ann steps close. "You'll stay in my second cabin. Off-grid. Only solar and wood heat. We never plant just for ourselves, remember?"

As we move to leave, the power flickers on—and off again.

A second later, a bullet shatters the cabin's front window.

We drop low. Caleb drags me behind the hearth. Ruth Ann is already pulling a rifle from behind the pantry wall.

The silence after the shot is worse than the sound itself.

They know where I am.

They didn't come to threaten.

They came to end it.
But we're still here.
Still breathing.
Still resisting.

Chapter Eight

THE VANISHING

Hampton Court Palace – May Nineteenth, 1521

By dawn, the book is gone.

The one Margaret swore never left our quarters. The one her mother bound in oilskin and hymns. The one written in the language no one but the women of her line could fully read.

Gone.

I search in silence. Not panic—not yet. Just the kind of stillness that comes before lightning strikes. I lift floorboards. Shake herb bundles. Run fingertips along the ledge behind the hearth.

Nothing.

Margaret watches me from the doorway. Her face is unreadable.

"You're sure?" I ask.

Her voice is a whisper. "I checked it last night."

There's no sign of forced entry. No scent out of place. No broken latch.

Which means someone used a key.

Or someone was invited.

Footsteps in the corridor.

Edward rushes in, out of breath, cheeks red.

"They took my satchel," he blurts. "The one with the spiral stone. And the tasting notes."

"Who?"

"I don't know! I left it in the practice chamber—"

Margaret's hands fly to her mouth. Her eyes blaze.

"You never leave the spiral unattended."

"I didn't mean to!" he shouts. "I was summoned—Lady Boleyn's maid said I was wanted in the kitchens. When I came back, it was gone!"

I cross the room in three quick strides and grip his shoulders—not hard, but firm enough that he goes still.

"This is not your fault," I say. "But we need truth. Did you see anyone?"

Edward hesitates.

Then: "Master Bainbridge was in the hall. He looked at me strangely."

Margaret turns away, one hand gripping the mantel like it might break under her fingers.

"That ledger is our blood," she says. "It has recipes my grandmother buried under coals to keep safe from witch-hunters. Notes from when childbirth was criminal. From when healing was burned."

Her voice shakes. "They'll rewrite it. Patent it. Twist it."

Edward's lip trembles. "I can remember most of it. I tried to memorize—"

She pulls him into her arms before he can finish.

My hands shake.

Because I know what comes next.

Once they have knowledge, they don't need the people who kept it.

They just need the brand.

The control.

Cromwell arrives before noon.

He doesn't knock.

He holds the satchel in one hand.

"Found this near the East Wing," he says smoothly. "Thought it might be yours."

Margaret's jaw tightens.

"It was locked inside a spice drawer," he adds. "One used only by the queen's apothecary."

A trap. Or a message.

Or both.

"Was anything missing?" Cromwell asks, all innocent court courtesy.

I glance at the satchel. The spiral stone is gone. The pages too old to replicate are gone.

They left the ones they could copy.

Calculated theft.

"What do you want, Thomas?" he says after a beat. "You play the loyal servant well. But that won't protect your family forever. If you're not with them, you're in the way."

"Who is 'them'?"

He smiles. "Whoever survives the next reign."

After he leaves, I burn rosemary and salt in the hearth. A ritual older than the court.

One my mother taught me the night before she was taken.

Margaret speaks the old words beneath her breath. Edward joins in, quietly.

We are a broken line.

But we are not finished.

That night, I write in the hidden ledger—not the stolen one, but the newer one, the one we keep inside the hollow of the ceiling beam.

The book is gone. Stolen, but not erased.

They think they hold the root.

But we are the soil.

And we will grow again.

Chapter Nine

THE RECKONING ROOM

Carter County, Tennessee — March Sixteenth, 2025 — 11:42 P.M.

The safe-house is nothing more than a converted hunting cabin on the backside of Roan Mountain. No address. No signal. Just a single solar panel and the smell of old cedar.

But tonight, it holds the last people who still believe the truth is worth bleeding for.

Ruth Ann, Caleb, and I crowd around the folding table. My laptop hums quietly, tethered to an encrypted hotspot beamed in from a drone miles away.

Across the screen: files. Evidence. Blood.

I click open a folder labeled **Jasper Clinic—Batch Logs**. Inside: shipping receipts, altered dosage sheets, physician kickback lists, and the last recorded death from a "non-lethal" dosage.

Marcus Tillery.

I stare at his file. At the timestamp.

It was signed off by someone who knew exactly what it would do.

Caleb watches me read, jaw tight.

"We have enough," I say. "We don't wait anymore."

He nods once. "Send it."

I hover over the key. But Ruth Ann grabs my hand.

"Not yet."

Her voice is iron wrapped in flannel.

"They'll kill you."

"I'm already on the list."

She shakes her head. "This isn't about martyrdom. This is about legacy. You send that file now, you spark a fire with no way back."

I close the laptop.

The fire in the hearth crackles. Outside, the wind rises. The mountains whisper through bare trees.

"What then?" I ask.

"We do it our way," she says. "Like Eleanor and Ezra. Like Jenny and your grandmother. We gather the circle."

She pulls out an old ledger—leather-bound, water-warped, written in three languages.

Not just records.

A roster.

Healers. Testers. Witnesses.

Mountain people with long memories and deeper roots.

"We call them," she says. "One by one. Quietly. Carefully."

Caleb leans forward. "You're talking about going public together."

"Not just public," she says. "Visible. Unignorable. Not one whistle-blower. A wall of them."

A reckoning.

A room they can't silence.

I nod.

Ruth Ann pours something from a tiny bottle into a cast-iron pan on the fire. A sweet, bitter scent rises—yarrow, pine, bloodroot.

A warning and a promise.

We begin to write.

Not just the report.

Not just the exposé.

The statement.

The testimony.

The story they tried to erase.

We sign it not with our names but with the spiral.

We remember.
We resist.
We return.

Chapter Ten

THE SPIRAL TURNS

Hampton Court Palace – May Twenty-First, 1521

Edward is gone when I wake.

His pallet is empty, the corner of the blanket folded with care. Not ripped away. Not rushed.

Chosen.

Margaret is already up, grinding valerian with a mortar and pestle, but her hands shake.

"He left this." She holds out a scrap of parchment, creased and smudged with sleep-smeared ink.

I'm safe. Don't follow. I'll watch and wait. I remember everything.

No signature. Just a spiral drawn in charcoal at the bottom.

He's telling us two things.

He's using what we taught him.

And someone's gotten to him.

I stagger to the washbasin, splash water on my face. The poison from three days ago still lingers in my joints, but this—

This is something worse.

"He's with her," I say. "Anne."

Margaret doesn't argue. "Cromwell wanted him where they could mold him. What better way than through a woman who knows how to manipulate power?"

"He thinks he's protecting us."

She nods. "He thinks he has to."

I sit at the table, spread out the few pages of the second ledger—the one we've kept hidden since the first was stolen. I flip to the passage I've read a hundred times this week.

Truth must be taught in silence and tested in fire. That which is stolen returns in another form.

It's a prayer. A prophecy. A warning.

The pages are brittle. The ink runs where rain got in once. But the words hold.

I press a finger to the spiral carved in the page's corner.

Then I look up.

"We end this."

Margaret meets my eyes.

"How?"

I open the hidden drawer beneath the hearth and pull out the silver tasting spoon—the original. The one passed down from the first Tester to leave the mountains for a crown.

"They've taken our book. Our child. Our knowledge."

I hold it tight.

"Now we give them what they fear most."

She knows what I mean.

The ritual.

The one never recorded in ink.

Passed mouth to mouth.

A way to bind memory to flesh.

To make truth live inside someone so completely, it cannot be extracted, erased, or denied.

"They'll kill you," she says.

"They'll try."

We begin preparing the herbs.

Foxglove in the smallest amount—just enough to sharpen.

Yarrow for clarity.

Thyme for protection.

And a drop of blood—mine.

When I sip the infusion, everything sharpens.

Voices I shouldn't hear echo through stone.

Candlelight pulses like a heartbeat.

And beneath it all, the spiral turns.

A knock at the door.

Margaret opens it.

Edward stands there, unharmed, but older in the eyes than he was yesterday.

"They think I belong to them," he says, voice like flint. "But I remembered who I am."

He steps forward and lays a vial on the table.

Inside: liquid the color of dusk.

"They were going to use this on you at tonight's feast."

I nod once.

Then pour it into the fire.

The room smells of copper and ruin.

But we are still standing.

And the spiral turns.

Chapter Eleven

FIRE IN THE HOLLOW

Carter County, Tennessee – March Seventeenth, 2025 – 3:38 A.M.

The knock comes soft, deliberate.

Not urgent.

That's how I know it's real.

I pull the bolt, crack the door, and find Caleb standing there with ash on his boots and smoke in his hair.

"It's started," he says.

My heart doesn't race. It tightens.

"How bad?"

He doesn't answer right away. Just pulls me outside.

From the ridge above the safehouse, we can see it—flames licking the sky above the old Tester barn. Orange against the dark like blood in water.

"They burned the archive," he says.

Ruth Ann joins us, binoculars raised.

"Not just burned. Erased. No sirens. No water run. No calls for help. This was sanctioned."

The barn had held the backups. Not digital—those were off-site— but the rest: paper maps, coded ledgers, seed samples, tinctures more than a century old.

Gone.

"This was a message," Caleb mutters.

"No," I say. "It was a mistake."

He looks at me.

"They think we put it all in one place. They think we're that naïve."

I pull out my phone.

No service. But that's not what I need.

I unlock the deadman's switch. The satellite queue loads.

A single file name: **SPIRAL_RECKONING.ZIP**

Caleb nods. "You sure?"

I press SEND.

We descend the ridge in silence.

When we reach the truck, Ruth Ann opens the glove box and pulls out an envelope. Inside: a handwritten list.

"Names of every reporter, professor, watchdog, and organizer we've worked with who still has a spine," she says. "You're not alone in this."

I look at the names. There are more than I thought.

They thought the fire would kill the truth.

But they didn't count on us scattering the embers.

Back at the safehouse, Sarah Walkingstick waits by the fire. She holds a satellite phone.

"Just got word," she says. "The files hit six inboxes before the trace locked out. One of them's printing in a news van outside Asheville right now."

I sit.

Breathe.

Then shake.

Because it's done.

There's no turning back.

Outside, the mountains wait.

Not in silence.

In memory.

And in flame.

Chapter Twelve

THE TASTE OF POWER

Hampton Court Palace – May Twenty-Second, 1521

The feast begins at dusk.

Tapestries ripple in the breeze from the Thames, perfumed candles mask the scent of sweat and ambition, and the tables groan with gold-draped abundance.

And every eye watches me.

Not the king.

Not the queen.

Me.

The man who drinks first.

The Tester.

I move from goblet to goblet. Sip. Wait. Nod.

I taste for bitterness, for heat, for too much nutmeg or not enough wine. I taste for death.

Tonight, everything tastes clean.

Too clean.

Margaret warned me. "They're not poisoning the wine anymore. They're testing you."

Testing loyalty.

Testing nerve.

Testing how far a man will go to keep his child safe.

At the head of the hall, Edward sits beside Lady Anne. His tunic is too fine, his posture too stiff, his eyes flicking to me every few seconds.

He is scared.

But he does not look away.

The final goblet is placed in my hand.

The king's.

Heavy. Ornate. Cool with expectation.

I lift it, tilt it, sip, and stop.

Because this one is not clean.

Not poison.

Memory.

The taste hits hard.

A tincture I know. A signature blend of Margaret's. One she used once, years ago, when my lungs collapsed in a frostsick field.

Mullein, licorice, and something bittersweet—

She sent this.

It's not an antidote.

It's a message.

Now.

The music swells. The courtiers laugh. And I drop the goblet.

Gasps. Movement. Guards shift.

I fall to my knees.

Not in pain.

In strategy.

Margaret moves before they do. She rushes forward, a vial in hand, and forces it to my lips.

Water.

But they don't know that.

Cromwell shouts. Harrington stands. Anne rises halfway, eyes wide.

The king only watches.

"What is it?" he demands.

Margaret's voice is steel. "He's been dosed. Not by wine. By hands that pass under your roof."

Silence spreads.

Then Cromwell steps forward.

"You play this game well," he says, not to her but to me. "But how long can you fake the fall?"

I meet his eyes from the floor.

"As long as I must."

He smiles.

"You'll wish you'd died tonight."

Margaret helps me to my feet. Her fingers grip my wrist hard—tight enough to bruise.

"Now," she whispers again. "The second ledger. You hid it?"

"Yes."

"Where?"

I glance at Edward.

He stands, too.

And from beneath his sleeve, he pulls the spiral stone.

He didn't lose it.

He never did.

He planted it in the queen's chamber.

With the copy of the ledger sewn into the hem of her prayer pillow.

A test within a test.

The spiral turns again.

And this time, it burns.

Chapter Thirteen

ASH AND INK

Carter County, Tennessee — March Eighteenth, 2025 —10:03 A.M.

The news breaks just after sunrise.

I don't see the broadcast live, but the screenshots hit every encrypted channel I follow.

"Pharmaceutical Giant Under Federal Investigation"

"Files Suggest Coordinated Targeting of Rural Communities"

"Appalachian Whistleblowers Link Tainted Trials to Overdose Spike"

I sit on the porch of Ruth Ann's second cabin with a mug of bone broth, the mug wrapped in both hands like it might ground me.

Caleb comes out carrying two more screenshots.

The first is of my face.

The second is of my grandmother's grave.

They've made us symbols.

And we're not dead yet.

Sarah texts a single word: **Held.**

That's all we need.

The press conference went forward.

The committee read the reports into the record.

And our story is now public domain.

Which means the next part of the fight begins.

I spend the day printing what we saved. Hard copies. Bound copies. Versions in three languages.

We seal them in fireproof envelopes. Store them in hollowed trees. Mail them to safe addresses.

We are not careless with truth anymore.

We scatter it like seeds.

That evening, Caleb brings out what's left of the 1894 box. Most of the vials are gone, distributed to trusted hands.

But the journal remains.

He places it between us on the table.

"Last page is for you," he says.

I open it.

The paper smells like cedar and oil. The binding crackles.

And there it is—blank space waiting for ink.

I uncap my pen.

And I write:

They tried to erase us, and they failed.

Because we remember not just the harm, but the healing.

We remember who taught us. What they burned. What they buried.

And we remember that memory is not passive.

It's resistance.

I sign it with the spiral.

The wind shifts.

Somewhere, a hawk cries.

And beneath the ridge, something very old stirs like it's waking up.

Because this isn't the end.

This is the remembering.

Chapter Fourteen

THE CROWN REMEMBERS

Hampton Court Palace – May Twenty-Third, 1521

They summon me at sunrise.

Not to the king's hall, but to the queen's.

Anne Boleyn stands before the hearth, her hands folded neatly, the spiral stone resting on the mantle beside her like a relic.

Edward kneels at her feet.

Not afraid, not proud.

Ready.

Margaret stands to one side, unblinking.

Guards line the walls, though their weapons remain sheathed. For now.

The queen gestures to the prayer cushion.

"I found something stitched inside," she says. "A ledger. Not the kind priests keep."

My pulse doesn't race. I won't give her that.

"I see," I say.

"You taught the boy well," she continues. "Even sewed it with golden thread. Clever."

Edward glances at me. Just once.

"I did not come here to punish you," Anne says.

My silence is its own answer.

She picks up the spiral stone, rolls it between her fingers.

"This symbol. It's older than your name. Older than the Testers. Do you know what it means?"

"It remembers," I say.

She nods. "That's what they told me too."

She moves to Margaret.

"You could be useful, you know. In my house. Not just testing. Advising. Women need their own healers. Especially women who plan to rule."

A dangerous offer.

Margaret's voice is quiet. "We don't serve crowns. We serve the living."

Anne smiles. "Then serve wisely. Because the crown remembers who aids it—and who does not."

She turns to Edward.

"You've seen how things work here. You've tasted it. Now choose. Stay at court. Be mine. Or leave with them and vanish."

The room holds its breath.

Edward looks at me.

Then at Margaret.

Then back to Anne.

He walks forward.

And kneels again—not to her, but beside her throne.

He opens his palm.

Inside it: a dried sprig of feverfew.

"For remembering," he says. "Not ruling."

Anne's eyes narrow. But she takes it.

The message is clear.

We will not disappear.

We will not be owned.

The spiral remains.

Even if we have to stitch it into the seams of the world.

Chapter Fifteen

WHAT REMAINS

Carter County, Tennessee – March Twenty, 2025 – Dusk

The fire pit crackles in the hollow below the ridge.

One by one, the circle gathers—some with canes, others with laptops, most with notebooks so worn the ink's been touched by three generations.

Healers. Testers. Midwives. Coders. Students. Elders.

Each with a sprig of yarrow in their hands.

Ruth Ann lights the central torch. Sarah sings the old hymn—half Cherokee, half Welsh, half grief.

I stand with Caleb at the edge, watching memory take form in firelight.

The files are out now.

The trials are starting.

The company issued a denial, then a second statement, then silence.

They'll pivot, rebrand, maybe collapse.

But the story won't die.

Because the roots are deeper than the rot.

We pass the spiral stone hand to hand. Not as symbol. As vow.

Not to preserve the past—but to carry it.

We record new entries in the old ledgers.

One for Jessica.

One for Marcus.

One for Amber.

And one for every name the system thought it could discard without witness.

The spiral turns again.

But this time, we turn with it.

We teach the children the taste of mint and copper. We show them how to blend elder with ash. We let them listen when the old ones speak of tinctures made in secret and how some poisons become protection when measured with care.

Later, alone at the cabin, I sit by the fire.

Edward's drawing herbs again—this time from memory.

He's humming a song Margaret once taught me.

I press my hand to the ledger's final page.

Not the end.

Just the latest entry.

We are not what they made us.

We are what we remembered in spite of them.

Then I close the book.

And let the flame burn just bright enough to write the next story in its light.

Chapter Sixteen

THE FINAL TASTING

Hampton Court Palace – May Twenty-Fourth, 1521

The hall is silent.

No music.

No murmured gossip behind goblets.

Only the rustle of silk and the slow, steady breath of a court that knows something has ended.

The king is not here.

Anne sits on the throne in his place.

Not crowned. Not yet.

But certain.

Margaret stands behind her, eyes narrowed, hands folded.

Edward is beside me, straight-backed, the spiral stone tucked inside his sleeve like a heartbeat.

I step forward.

One last goblet.

One last taste.

I lift the cup. I sip.

And I smile.

Because this one is clean.

No bitterness.

No threat.

Only wine.

Only memory.

Anne watches. "Well?"

"No poison," I say. "Not today."

She nods once. "Then we move forward."

And we do.

Not with banners or bells.

But with knowledge carried in the blood.

With recipes passed mouth to mouth.

With truth no longer hidden in hollow beams.

Later, I walk the palace garden alone.

Margaret joins me without a word.

We pause beneath the ash tree Edward marked when we arrived.

"I've written everything," I say. "Even the parts I swore I wouldn't."

She nods. "So have I."

"He knows enough now."

She smiles. "He knows more than we did when we started."

The sun slips behind the towers.

Somewhere in the kitchens, a new Tester is being trained—not to serve, but to protect.

We don't need thrones.

We need memory.

And someone to taste the future before the crown drinks it.

Chapter Seventeen

ROOTBOUND

Carter County, Tennessee — March Twenty-Fourth, 2025

Spring arrives late in these ridges, but fast once it finds a foothold.

The yarrow pushes through frost-softened earth like it's answering a summons.

I walk the boundary line behind my grandmother's house with Edward, now tall enough to meet my gaze without tilting his chin.

A spiral stone in one hand. A trowel in the other.

We stop where the creek bends sharp around a white oak.

"This is where she used to leave the offerings," I say.

Edward nods. He digs carefully, placing each clump of earth to the side.

We plant seeds wrapped in cloth—wormwood, vervain, mountain mint.

He presses them in like a prayer.

"These are for remembering," he says.

"Yes."

"And these?" He holds up the next bundle—dark, bitter seeds wrapped in red thread.

"For protection."

He buries those deeper.

We mark the spot with a stone etched in the old pattern. Not carved, but pressed—spiral into soft rock, like my grandmother taught me.

Later, on the porch, Caleb joins us.

He's holding a parcel.

"The first printed copy," he says. "Off the press this morning."

The cover reads:

The Testers: What the Poison Remembered

Inside: every name, every note, every vanished voice we could recover.

Edward opens to the dedication. His voice catches as he reads aloud:

For those who swallowed the fire to keep others whole.

For those who remembered when silence was safer.

For those who turned knowing into healing.

And for those still learning how.

Ruth Ann calls from the truck—she's headed to the library in town. First box of books to donate.

Sarah's already speaking at the university clinic.

And the mountain?

The mountain holds us like it always has.

Not in stone.

In seed.

In water.

In the way grief bends into teaching.

Edward closes the book and places it beside the seeds we've yet to plant.

He looks at me.

"We're not done, are we?"

"No," I say. "We're just rootbound. For now."

Chapter Eighteen

THE SPIRAL CARVES DEEP

Hampton Court Palace — May Twenty-Fifth, 1521

They send for me at twilight.

Not the king.

Not Anne.

Cromwell.

A parchment arrives, folded with precision, bearing only a seal—a spiral, pressed into wax.

Not royal.

Ours.

I follow the corridor beneath the old cloisters, past the chapel, into the rooms no courtier speaks of.

When I arrive, Cromwell is waiting beside a single candle and an opened book.

Not the stolen ledger, but the original—the one I thought was lost.

He doesn't speak for a while.

Just runs his fingers along the pages.

"You knew we'd keep copies," I say quietly.

"I did. But I needed to see what you would do without it."

"To see if we were dangerous?"

He closes the book.

"To see if you were faithful."

I step closer. "To what?"

"To the crown. To the old ways. To each other. Faith is measured in silence, not vows."

He holds the book out.

"Anne has plans," he says. "For this court. For this kingdom. She wants the power of healing. Not for mercy. For strategy. For legacy."

"She wants control."

"She wants survival."

I take the book.

The leather is warm. Familiar.

It feels like holding a heartbeat.

"She'll use us," I say.

"Yes," he agrees. "But she won't break you."

"And the boy?"

"He's still yours—but walks both paths now."

That's the price.

Not exile.

Not execution.

Inclusion.

Bound by oaths they'll never write down.

I nod.

Cromwell steps back into the shadows.

As I leave, I feel the spiral shift inside me.

Not turn.

Carve.

This court won't kill us.

It will use us.

And if we're clever—we'll let it.

Until the next page needs writing.

Chapter Nineteen

THE HOLLOW TESTAMENT

Carter County, Tennessee – March Twenty-Eighth, 2025 – 4:17 A.M.

The sky hasn't lightened yet, but I'm already walking the creek-line behind Ruth Ann's cabin.

Soaked boots. Dirty hands. Wide eyes.

The world feels like it's waiting.

I reach the hollow beneath the ash tree—the same one Edward marked, the one that held a ledger once buried, now bound and printed.

I kneel and dig.

Not out of fear.

Out of ritual.

Inside the hollow: a cedar box wrapped in waxed cloth.

I open it.

Inside, a single notebook—blank and heavy.

This one's for what comes next.

I thumb the first page and write:

We did not win. We survived.

We did not silence the harm. We sang over it.

We did not end them. We outlived their version of us.

Footsteps crunch behind me.

Edward sits cross-legged in the leaves, the spiral stone in his lap.

"You going to tell them the whole thing?" he asks.

I look down at the page.

"Yes. Even the parts that hurt."

He nods. "Then I'll help."

He pulls out his own notebook. A smaller one. Bound with red string.

"I've been writing too," he says.

Of course he has.

We don't inherit the mountain by name.

We inherit it by remembering.

And by testifying.

By sunrise, we've written four more pages.

Warnings. Recipes. Maps.

Truths no algorithm can predict.

Edward caps his pen and looks toward the blue line of dawn.

"They'll come again, won't they?"

I nod. "They always do."

"But we'll be ready."

Not a question.

A statement.

We reseal the cedar box, hands pressed to its lid.

Leave it for the ones who'll need it next.

Because memory is never finished.

And neither are we.

Chapter Twenty

TASTED, REMEMBERED, CARRIED

Hampton Court Palace – May Thirty, 1521

The spiral is now etched into the king's seal.

Anne had it pressed into wax beside the royal crest during yesterday's proclamation.

No one says it aloud, but they see it.

And they whisper.

I taste the wine at the coronation feast.

Not out of duty anymore.

Out of witness.

Edward hands me the goblet—now in court colors, hair combed back, palms steady.

He watches me drink.

I nod.

Clean.

We eat beneath banners stitched with red and gold.

The room swells with song and soft deception.

Anne sits beside the king. She wears no crown yet, but she doesn't need one.

Not anymore.

She has the book now.

Not the original, not even a copy—just the knowledge.

Inside her.
Inside all of us who refused to let it die.
Later, in our chambers, Margaret opens the new ledger.
At last.
The one we'll never hide.
The one written in three hands now.
She asks, "What do we call this chapter?"
Edward answers.
"The one where we lived."
We write:
We were the last line and the first memory.
We tasted what others feared.
We carried it so they wouldn't have to.
The spiral turns again.
But this time, it doesn't carve.
It roots.
And we are ready.

Chapter Twenty-One

THE SEED BELOW THE ASH

Carter County, Tennessee — April First, 2025 — New Moon

No moon tonight.

Just stars.

And fire.

We gather on the ridge—thirty strong, maybe more.

Some carry jars of salve, others flash drives, others just memory.

The broadcast begins in an hour.

An Appalachian oral history collective. A national health justice podcast. A university archive. A rural medicine conference.

All going live at once.

Our story won't just be told.

It will echo.

Edward stands beside me, lantern in one hand, notebook in the other.

Caleb has the hard drive with the final files: testimony, treatment data, soil memory maps, and the names of every healer the ledgers remembered.

We walk to the place where we buried the cedar box.

We dig—not to unearth, but to plant beside it.

A sealed envelope, inside: this generation's entry.

Written by all three of us.

Signed with the spiral.

We place it in the earth. Cover it gently.

Because this isn't the end.

This is inheritance.

Seed, not tomb.

Later, as the signal goes live and the first story begins to stream through the dark, I press my hand to the dirt.

I think.

Of ledger ink and fire. Of foxglove and feverfew.

Of all we lost and all we learned.

And I whisper, for whoever finds this next:

We tasted what they poisoned.

We remembered what they erased.

We planted what they feared.

Now it's your turn.

Chapter Twenty-Two

TESTAMENT

Somewhere Between

There is no date for this.

No place name.

Just breath, and ink, and memory.

This is for the ones who come after.

The ones who find the stones carved in spiral.

The ones who open the hollow logs and light the cedar bundles and whisper the words they were never taught aloud.

This is for you.

You are not starting the story.

You are not finishing it either.

You are walking into it.

You are the echo of every woman who wrapped yarrow in her hem and bled through the trial.

You are the breath of every man who swallowed ash so his child wouldn't taste it.

You are the last drop in the goblet, and the one who refused to sip.

You are the tester and the tasted.

The wound and the salve.

You are the memory that refused to burn.

We did not write this book to be sacred.

We wrote it to be useful.
Use it.
Taste carefully.
Pass it on.
And remember—
The spiral does not end.
It turns.

Chapter Twenty-Three

LEDGER

(Unnumbered Pages – Undated)

Jessica Winters

Age: twenty-four

Prescription: Northeastern Medical Oxyproxil, 20mg

Injury: Torn rotator cuff, factory line work

Outcome: Overdose, March twelve, 2025

Notes: Requested reduction in dosage. Physician declined. Last words to mother: "It's too much, but they won't listen."

Status: Entered. Witnessed.

Marcus Tillery

Age: twenty-two

Prescription: Northeastern Medical Oxyproxil XR, 40mg

Injury: Construction site collapse, vertebral compression

Outcome: Found unresponsive. Died en route.

Notes: Attempted taper. Refilled higher dose without request.

Status: Entered. Witnessed.

Amber Collins

Age: nineteen

Prescription: Oxyproxil starter sample, 10mg escalating

Injury: Warehouse back strain

Outcome: Fatal respiratory depression, March thirteen, 2025

Notes: Labeled "non-compliant" after questioning side effects.

Status: Entered. Witnessed.

Jenny Blackwood

Age: thirty-one

Prescription: Withdrawn prior to death

Injury: Degenerative disc

Outcome: Presumed suicide. Family disputes.

Notes: Herbal protocols documented in children's books.

Status: Entered. Witnessed.

Ezra Tester

Died: 1992

Occupation: Herbalist, unlicensed

Legacy: Preserved 1894 vial. Protected spiral ledger.

Notes: Buried warning with Eleanor Walkingstick.

Status: Entered. Witnessed.

Eleanor Walkingstick

Died: 1903

Occupation: Midwife, Healer, Tester

Legacy: Originated hybrid ledger script. Taught "Taste, Map, Remember."

Notes: Survived cholera outbreak by mapping contaminated wells.

Status: Entered. Witnessed.

Dr. Grace Blackwood

Born: 1990

Occupation: Researcher, whistleblower, descendant

Action: Released files March eighteen, 2025

Notes: Survived attempted erasure. Taught Edward Tester.

Status: Entered. Witnessed.

Edward Tester

Born: 2017

Occupation: Heir. Witness. Scribe.

Notes: Spiral passed. Memory held.

Status: Still Writing. Still Witnessing.

Let this ledger grow.

Not with names of the fallen alone.

But with those who stood between the poison and the cup.

Chapter Twenty-Four

THE VAULT BENEATH THE CROWN

Windsor Castle – May Thirty-First, 1521

The tunnel beneath the east wing is colder than the grave.

No guards. No torches. Just a staircase cut into black stone, slick with water and silence.

Edward moves before me through the dark.

He knows the path better than I do.

Because he dreamed it.

Two nights ago, he returned to the safehouse after hours alone in the woods. His clothes were mud-streaked, his face tear-stained but resolved. When he fell asleep, he woke screaming—not in fear but in recognition.

"I saw the lock," he said. "And the door. And the woman inside. And the spiral wasn't carved. It was alive."

Anne didn't question him. She didn't demand explanation or proof.

She just handed him the stone and whispered:

"Then it's time."

Now we move through the dark beneath Windsor.

Hinged corridors. Soot-stained air. Paintings long removed. No sounds but our footsteps.

Until we reach it. A wall with no handle.

No hinge.

Just a spiral—etched in shallow relief across stone.

Edward lifts the stone from his pouch. Presses it to the carving.

The wall hums beneath our hands.

Then opens.

Inside: a single chamber. Low light. White walls. A single bed.

A woman.

Margaret's mother.

Alive.

She's hooked to a system of tubes and tinctures. Vials that glow faintly with substances I don't recognize. Her eyes are open, but vacant —looking through us rather than at us.

Edward takes one step toward her.

She gasps—like a breath she's been holding for years finally broke.

"Tester," she says. "The blood is here."

Edward kneels beside her. His hands shake as he reaches for hers.

"I'm here," he whispers. "It's me. Edward."

Her fingers twitch against his.

"They took everything."

"Not everything."

He reaches into his coat and pulls out the scroll Anne gave him.

Unrolls it. Places it in her palm.

The words glow faintly in the chamber's low light. Like the paper remembers her touch.

She exhales.

A single tear tracks down her weathered cheek.

"I knew you'd come."

I stay back, by the door.

Because this is no longer my journey. This is between blood.

Between generations.

Between those who carry the same memory through different vessels.

I keep watch, hand on my blade, ears straining for any sign we've been discovered. The king's guards patrol the east wing regularly. Anne helped us time our entry between rotations, but we have minutes at most.

"Edward," I warn softly. "We must be quick."

He doesn't acknowledge me. He's whispering something to his grandmother, head bent close to hers. Her expression shifts from vacancy to focus, eyes sharpening with each word he speaks.

Then her gaze snaps to me.

"They're listening."

"What?"

"In the walls," she hisses, voice sudden and urgent. "They don't need guards anymore. They hear the blood."

I turn—too late.

A chime sounds throughout the chamber.

Not an alarm. A heartbeat. Amplified. Tracked.

Doors hiss open across the vault.

Steps.

Fast.

Heavy.

Anne's warning echoes in my head:

"If he's not out in ten minutes, he's not getting out."

Edward turns, face set in determination beyond his years.

"I'm not leaving her."

"Edward—"

"I'm not."

His grandmother grips his hand with surprising strength.

And whispers something into his ear—words I cannot hear, passed from age to youth, from keeper to carrier.

He freezes.

Then stands.

Eyes burning with purpose.

Voice clear as bell metal.

"She stays. But she gives us the last sequence."

"I'm taking the Archive Code."

. . .

He places the stone against the slab at the foot of her bed.

The floor opens with a mechanical groan.

A drawer slides forward.

Inside:

– A bone scroll case.

– A small dagger with a spiral hilt.

– A single lock of hair—red and gray twined together.

– And a word burned into the wood: **REMEMBER**

He grabs the case. Tucks the dagger into his belt. Leaves the hair—some things are not meant to travel.

Footsteps thunder closer, voices calling commands.

He turns to me, face set in the same expression Margaret wore when she pushed us through the grate.

"We run."

We do.

Through the dark.

Back into the spiral.

And into the war that waits.

His grandmother watches us go. Her eyes—suddenly clear, suddenly present—hold no fear for herself. Only certainty that what matters most has been preserved.

As the door closes behind us, I hear her begin to sing.

A Welsh lullaby, the same one Margaret sang to Edward as an infant.

The one that taught him herb lore in melody before he could speak.

We flee through passages that should be unfamiliar but somehow aren't. Edward leads with uncanny certainty, the Archive Code clutched against his chest. When we reach a fork, he doesn't hesitate—left, then right, then up a stairwell I would have missed entirely.

Behind us, voices echo. Boots on stone. The rattle of weapons.

"How do you know the way?" I gasp as we sprint through a corridor lined with empty portrait frames.

"I don't," he says. "The stone does."

We emerge into night air—a servant's entrance on the castle's northern face, unguarded because it's meant to be unopenable from the outside.

Stars wheel overhead, ancient and indifferent to the secrets we've stolen.

Edward stops at the edge of the surrounding forest, turning back to look at the castle that held his grandmother prisoner for years while we thought her dead.

"We'll come back for her," he promises.

And somehow, I believe him.

Because Edward is no longer just my son.

He's a keeper.

EPILOGUE

The Keeper's Legacy

Carter County, Tennessee — One Year Later

The hearing room falls silent as I approach the podium.

The congressional oversight committee looks down from their elevated platform—twelve faces ranging from bored to hostile to genuinely concerned.

I place my materials on the podium: research files, death certificates, the USB drive containing Ezra's data. And lastly, the journal—now appearing as a simple leather-bound notebook filled with handwritten observations.

"Dr. Blackwood," begins Senator Williams, "you've made serious allegations against Northeastern Medical. Yet there were irregularities with your research materials when federal agents conducted their investigation."

I nod.

"There were indeed irregularities, Senator. Though not with my research."

I open a folder containing photographs: local cemeteries with clusters of identical death dates. Medicine cabinets filled with identical prescriptions. Charts showing dosage increases that follow no medical protocol.

"The irregularity," I continue, "is with a system that allows companies to target vulnerable communities, then bury the resulting overdose data."

I present the first series of exhibits—patient charts with identical dosage increases despite different conditions, ages, and weights.

In the back of the room, Harrison watches, face impassive. But I can see the subtle tells—the slight flare of nostrils, the tightened jaw. He knows what's coming.

"This isn't coincidental, Senator. This is methodical."

Behind me, Ruth Ann sits with perfect posture, eyes forward. Beside her, Caleb—the marks beneath his skin now faded to a pattern like memory itself. Sarah Walkingstick flanked by elders from three counties. A circle gathered, just as they had in Branwen's cottage five centuries before.

I press my hand to the journal, feeling its warmth.

"My research uncovered a pattern that stretches back centuries," I explain. "Companies that profit from pain consistently target communities with limited access to care. They systematically discredit traditional knowledge that might compete with patented formulations."

Harrison stands, whispering urgently to a committee aide. I don't pause.

"We found evidence that Northeastern Medical documented a non-addictive pain formula derived from native plants—a formula that preliminary trials proved more effective than opioid-based treatments. Three months later, the researcher died of an 'accidental overdose' despite having no history of drug use."

I look directly at Harrison.

"The same pattern claimed my grandmother. And Jennifer Tester. And dozens of others whose deaths were classified as misuse rather than predictable outcomes of predatory prescribing."

"Dr. Blackwood," says Senator Lee, leaning forward, "are you suggesting deliberate elimination of researchers who threatened their market?"

"I'm providing evidence of it, Senator."

I display the final exhibit—emails discussing the need to *"contain potential market disruption"* from Ezra's research and to *"manage the Tester situation with maximum discretion."*

The room erupts in whispers. Harrison exits abruptly, phone pressed to his ear.

Later, as reporters swarm the steps outside, Ruth Ann takes my arm.

"They'll fight back," she warns.

"Let them," I say. "We've got something they don't."

"What's that?"

I touch the spiral stone at my throat.

"Memory."

That night, I walk alone to the hollow oak where Edward first buried the ledger. Where Anne hid the Archive Code. Where five centuries of resistance bloomed from a single seed of defiance.

I kneel at the base of the tree. Dig until my fingers touch oilskin.

Inside, just as it was when Margaret wrapped it: the ledger. Intact. Breathing.

But now, new pages have grown from its spine.

I trace the words with soil-stained fingers. Stories that weren't written yet, somehow already remembered. Grief that hadn't been born, somehow already mourned. Victory that wasn't yet won, somehow already celebrated.

I read the final entry, written in a hand I recognize but have never seen:

From Thomas Tester, Royal Taster, 1521
To Grace Blackwood, Truth Taster, 2025

The spiral remembers when we cannot.
What they could not break, they tried to bury.
What they could not control, they tried to poison.
But some things survive being swallowed.
In our blood.

In our bones.
In the way children taste danger before it's named.
In every court, in every century, someone profits from poison.
And someone must stand between the chalice and the crown.

I place my hand on the soil as the spiral stone at my throat warms against my skin.

The circle doesn't close.

It turns.

It remembers.

It waits.

And somewhere far away, I feel a boy's hand reach across time to touch the same earth—Edward, placing the Archive Code to rest, knowing someone would find it when the pattern repeated.

When poison took a new form.

When the tester was needed again.

I brush dirt from the ledger and rise.

Behind me, the light from Ruth Ann's cabin cuts through gathering dusk.

Voices drift down the slope—Caleb, Sarah, the circle expanding.

I turn away from the oak.

Not finished.

Just beginning.

Because in every court, in every century, someone profits from poison.

And someone must stand between the chalice and the crown.

THE END

Free book-club guides @ genescottbooks.com